Out Behind the Barn

by

John Boden & Chad Lutzke

- publishing -

OUT BEHIND THE BARN

1

As the sun fell tired, the boys lay on their beds. The younger of the two watched a spider on the ceiling, skittering across the peeling paint above him. He wondered if one night the spider might drop and crawl down his throat while sleeping, but didn't have the heart to end its life. His older brother tossed a ball up at the paint, chipping away what was already dead.

The sound of the truck drew their attention away from the spider and the paint, and they spun onto their bellies and peered through the drapes, keeping them closed around their noses so as not to belie the fact they were peeping. Miss Maggie always scolded them for being nosy, telling them nosy people lose their noses for real in accidents. Then she'd lean in and pinch their noses and laugh that witchy laugh.

The truck turned at the end of the lane and bounced towards the farm house. Davey smiled and held the curtain between tight fingers. The truck groaned to a stop near the barn and Maggie got out. She was singing as she stomped her way to the doors and slid them aside. She was always singing— unheard lyrics through whispered breath that sounded like hexes or prayers. As she turned back to the truck, she caught sight of the boys peering. Her face split with a smile and she waggled a boney finger at them. They closed the curtain and faced one another. Ronny gasped and inched away from the window.

"We in trouble, Davey?" young Ronny asked.

"Nah, she was smilin'. She don't smile when she's mad. Now that I think on it, I don't think I ever seen her mad."

Ronny crept back to the window, one eye peeking through the gap in the curtains. Maggie had hoisted something from the back of the truck and was carrying it into the barn. It was long and big, and the weight of it stooped her aging back. She stopped to flick a switch and rafter lights spilled from the building. In that light, Davey saw an arm fall from the side of the bundle. He smiled.

"She got someone!"

The children both grinned and settled in their beds, eyes fixed to the ceiling again. This time they stared through the paint and through the webs and daydreamed about a future with the visitor, maybe another boy their age. A brother.

"I've been prayin' she would," Ronny said. "Do you think they'll like us?"

"If Miss Maggie lets them in the house, they'll take to us. Without a doubt. We'll show them the ropes."

Talk gave way to heavy lids and tired tongues, and sleep came while the night was a quiet quilt stitched together by the old woman's singing, the crickets, and the dull hum of the barn lights.

2

Davey stood in the bedroom doorway and watched the woman sleep. It hadn't been a boy after all—a brother nor a sister—but a young woman. Maybe in her late twenties, early thirties. Fit and thin of arm. Her hair a ginger nest of braids. She wore a light-colored dress with buttons to her neck. Miss Maggie made them all keep their tops buttoned tight and high, to hide the scars. The woman's chest puffed with small breaths while she slept. A large blue bump sat perched in the middle of her forehead, a dark red scab nested in its center.

"She must've used the hammer," Davey muttered to himself, then turned to go eat breakfast.

The boys sat on opposite sides of the table, sipping on orange juice and waiting for their food. They stared across the room and out the screen door, watching Maggie as she stood on the porch, shredding the clothing. She held the garden shears in one arthritic hand and tore long swatches of fabric from garments in a basket—a blue dress, a pair of socks, panties, and a white blouse. When she was finished, all was reduced to a few yards of streamer-sized scrap cloth. Maggie settled the basket on her hip and began the lap of the property, stopping every so many feet to tie a piece of cloth to the fence, or nail it to a tree. She then returned to the porch where she dropped the empty basket and

9

leaned far to the right until her hip popped. She groaned at the sound, then turned and headed into the house.

"You boys glad to be done with school?" Maggie asked as she gathered their empty glasses.

Ronny nodded with vigor, Davey just shrugged.

"We home school. Doesn't seem to be a whole lotta difference." Davey held his glass out to her. She took it but stopped and put a finger to her chin, thinking.

"Hold summer in your hand or pour summer in a glass. Change the season in your veins by raising glass to lip and titling summer in." She smiled and her old eyes twinkled. Tiny stars in pools of dark honey.

Davey nodded and smiled. "Bradbury?"

"Indeed," she replied, as she poured boiling water over oats.

"I believe he's my favorite."

The boys went statue-still when the young woman came out of the bedroom. She said nothing as she eased herself into the chair at the head of the table. She'd been sleeping for two days and uttered not a word since her arrival.

Maggie came from the kitchen and set bowls of oatmeal down before them. "Eat up, boys." She winked at Ronny as she handed him a glass of chocolate milk. "Or I'll beat you with a stick," she added and tickled his neck, causing him to giggle and squirm. Davey laughed and began to eat.

The woman sat still and stared at the bowl before her. Maggie returned with a plate of blueberry muffins and placed a hand on the woman's slumped

10

shoulder.

"If you don't feel up to it yet, hon', go lie down and rest yourself. We won't mind." She kissed the top of her head and the woman scooted out of her chair and made her way down the hall and back to her room. They heard the bed springs squeal as she lay down, and after a few moments they resumed eating.

"She's a slow one, huh?" Davey asked.

"She'll be ready when she's ready, Dear. Now mind your meal or I'll toss you in the oven and bake you up nice an' crisp."

Both the boys giggled, then filled themselves with muffins, oats, and chocolate milk.

3

Ronny sat on the floor watching the television, giggling at the blue cat chasing the little brown mouse while Davey slouched in the sagging chair, dozing, a worn Zane Grey book in his lap. Maggie was on the porch. She stared up at the bruising sky and took a drag on her cigarette. She had had such grand plans for herself, destined for greatness. A degree in anthropology and a teaching slot at the local college. And she did that, but the job atrophied into a temporary position, then faded away altogether. She spent so much time alone with her books. So many years in self-imposed solitude. Years shaved from her like whiskers.

She would have gone mad, had it not been for the boys. Her boys. She watched the sun slink behind the mountain and smoked her Marlboro down to the filter. She reckoned it was a visual metaphor and grimly smiled.

The sound of cartoon screams and quiet chuckles poked her ears through the porch screen door. Her smile widened and smoke leaked from her thin lips. Yes. She would have gone mad.

4

The boys broke from their chores and swung on the porch, being careful not to swing too hard. Miss Maggie frowned upon the bang of wood against the house. The boys were watching Maggie as she schooled the woman on clothespins and the simple way they work. Maggie's hands guided the woman's own, and after so many failed attempts, the woman clipped a single sock by herself. Ronny cheered but the woman remained expressionless. She was relearning. They had seen it before.

"She's doing quite well, ain't she?" Maggie said, climbing the porch stairs with winded breath.

"Yes ma'am," Davey said.

"Do you boys want to help her finish the load while I bake that pie I promised?"

Ronny tore from the swing, Davey soon after, then stopped short and turned. "What kinda pie?"

Maggie touched a crooked finger to her chin and pretended to think hard: "Mmmm...how about rabbit turd and gopher guts?"

Davey laughed, "Yuck. No really?!"

"Blackberry with sugar crust."

"That's better." The boy rushed to catch up to his brother.

"She's struggling with the shirts so just stick with the socks and the underwear," Maggie said.

"What's her name?" Ronny asked.

"That's Miss Rose."

"Hello, Miss Rose," the two said in almost unison.

There was no reply. Her lips seemed to try to make a smile, or a grimace. The line of her mouth became a wavy one.

Ronny frowned, and as usual, Davey took to cheering him up.

"She'll come around. She's rusty is all. And we're the oil."

Ronny believed his older brother and showed it with a smile. A smile full of naivety and innocence, optimism and blissful ignorance.

Maggie read to the boys while they sprawled across the floor, changing positions every so often as the hard wood overstayed its welcome against their ankle bones, knobbed knees, and elbows. Miss Rose sat in a chair nearby, listening intently to the stories being told. Poe, Bradbury, and the occasional Brothers Grimm tale were the customary. The boys found such fascination in the otherworldly, the unimaginable, and especially curious of Poe's own fear of being buried alive.

"But it didn't happen often, right?" Ronny asked with concern.

"No, not often," Maggie said. "But there were times when ailments came along and gave the impression of death. In times before we resuscitated, or knew of it. And those poor souls would find themselves awakened on a table while their fluids ran out of them, formaldehyde rushin' in. Or right during dissection even, while the blade split the skin. But worst of all, some would awaken with the earth on them, six feet from the rest of the world, no one hearing their screams."

"B...but, that don't happen no more, right?" Ronny asked. Davey sat wide-eyed, needing to hear the same answer Ronny searched for.

"No, hon'. Not anymore. We make sure people are good and dead before we pile on the dirt. Good and dead."

"More than just breath on a mirror?" Davey asked.

"Much more."

The boys drew a collective sigh, while Miss Rose got up from her chair, went to her room and shut the door.

"I'll bet tomorrow's the day," Ronny said.

"If she's ready," said Maggie.

The boys headed for bed with bellies full of milk and heads full of Poe and his irrational fears.

"I knew it," Ronny said. "Davey, I knew it! Look!" He pointed at the window and to the ground below where Miss Rose hung clothes on the line, all by herself.

"Let's go talk to her." Davey said.

The two bounded down the stairs and through the house, stopping at the screen door. Davey was worried. Not for himself but for Ronny. What if Miss Rose didn't like them. Ronny took too easily to visitors, invested too much before they had a chance to know him. Before they even knew themselves.

"She might not talk, Ronny. She might be a bad one altogether."

"She's not. I can tell."

"How can you tell?"

"Her eyes. They see the world how I see it. There's a twinkle in them, like they've got love to give."

Davey didn't know much about any of that. He just knew about protecting and hurting, and without one would come the other. Sometimes more than he felt they could bear. Davey held the screen door open and let Ronny pass through, like this was more for him. Ronny walked up to Miss Rose and took to talking right away.

"Good morning, Miss Rose. We've been watching you, and I just wanna say I think you're doin' real good."

Miss Rose stopped with the laundry, turned to Ronny and knelt down. "Thank you, Davey. It's hard. I can't remember how to do these things. Like I never knew them at all. I had to think hard about walking and standing, everything. Like I was a child again." She made a face as though that sudden glut of words pouring from her had been exhausting. She looked at the smaller boy and smiled, "I'll be alright, though."

"I'm Ronny, that's Davey. Come here, Davey."

Davey didn't hurry over, he strolled. And on the way, he thought about things. About past visitors and what made each one what and how would this one be compared to others. You could say he had his guard up, for the both of them.

"Good morning, Miss Rose. I think you're doing a fine job, too." Davey held his hand out to offer a shake. Miss Rose's skin was pale and dotted with freckles. Smooth and taut, not loose and callused. And when he touched her, there was energy there. Nothing supernatural or unnatural, just an attraction he couldn't well understand. Like static. And it wasn't sexual. It just was. Before letting go, he stroked his thumb across the meat of her hand to feel that smoothness once more, and his belly filled with daddy long legs that scurried about madly long after he let go.

The three ate breakfast together while Maggie sat and observed. She always kept a close eye, especially when it came to her boys. If anything ever happened to them, the world couldn't hold all the tears that'd fall. She stoked these thoughts as she pretended to read the cereal box before her, then was dragged from them when Davey started speaking of a cartoon he'd watched about a land of balloon people and the terrible pincushion man who came to terrorize them.

Their talk at the table was short and simple. The boys knew not to ask too much of Miss Rose this early on. They understood that she still wasn't the her that she'd one day be.

"I see you've done quite well with the laundry, Miss Rose," Maggie said.

"Thank you. It's an easy enough chore. Even if it did take a bit to get these to work how they should." She held out her smooth, pale hands and Davey thought about touching them. To feel that static again. "I really had to think on it."

"I think I'll have the boys take you out today. Show you around a bit, stretch your legs."

"I'd like that." Miss Rose smiled at the boys and slowly winked a hazel eye. And the spiders came back to live in Davey's belly.

"Sometimes you'll find a good and ripe one already on the ground, before the rot gets it," Davey said, as he felt through the grass under the apple tree.

Ronny was in the middle of the tree, surrounded by winding branches, foraging for the perfect red fruit to give their new friend. Miss Rose watched with child-like wonder as Ronny would reach for an apple, then turn it, only to find it wasn't quite red.

"I think I love apples," Miss Rose said.

"I know I do," Ronny said. "I like the way the skin sticks between my teeth sometimes."

"Miss Maggie makes applesauce with the apples from this very tree," Davey added.

"And sometimes I eat the seeds so's I can feel them here." Ronny rubbed his stomach. "But don't tell Miss Maggie. She says they'll grow a tree in my belly."

"Our secret," Miss Rose said.

"I found one!" Davey yelled. He wiped the apple off on his pant leg and handed it to Miss Rose. "Twist the stem and make a wish."

Miss Rose looked at the apple with confusion on her face.

"Like this." Davey held the apple and mocked twisting the stem. "Then make a wish. Anything you want. If the stem breaks on the third twist then your wish will come true."

Miss Rose took the apple and closed her eyes. The

two boys watched with anticipation. Her wish seemed to go on forever. Then she startled them both with a sudden twist of the stem that popped off into her hand. There was silence after that, as though paying their respects to the dead wish.

"I wished for ..."

In a panic, Davey interrupted her. "Don't say the wish! Maybe there's still a chance."

Ronny jumped down from the tree and stood next to her. "It's okay. There'll be more wishes."

Maggie watched her boys from a nearby path. She watched them express concern, sympathy. And maybe even love. A love that she selfishly, ashamedly felt should be reserved for her only, their mother. She stubbed out her cigarette on the bark of the nearest tree and dropped the butt in her sweater pocket. She sourly grimaced at the fact the jealousy hadn't been stubbed out as well.

"Read the one about the kids and the electric grandmother!"

"Do you never tire of Bradbury, my boys?" Maggie smiled and dragged her fingers across the spines that lined the shelf. Finding the title she sought, she pulled the book free and made her way back to her chair. The boys sat in anticipation of a story they'd heard more than once, but each time was like the first. Most stories were like that for them. It didn't matter how many times they'd heard them. Even the most familiar was always welcome, like a hungry man who tires of steak, well fed and bloated, only to crave more later.

After the evening story, the boys tucked themselves in, the moon spilling onto their beds.

"Davey?" Ronny's voice was small in the big quiet room.

"Yeah?"

"I'm sad sometimes."

"Everyone is, Ronny."

"Sometimes I'm real happy, almost always, but then it's like someone opens a window and instead of rain coming in it's sad and I feel real bad for a little while."

Davey clicked on his bedside lamp and looked sideways at his brother. The moonlight went in hiding. "It happens to me too sometimes. But I think it's probably normal."

"Think I'm growing up?" Ronny sat up and there was a twinkle of excitement in his eyes.

"Sure you are," Davey replied, and hoped it contained enough assuredness to pass as truth.

"I can't wait to be big and grown up." Ronny laid back down and the room settled back into its quiet. Davey snatched a book from his nightstand and began to read, Ronny in his bed smoothing the hair of his stuffed bear. Unable to focus, Davey closed the book and dropped it on the floor beside his bed with a thump.

"She sure is something," Davey said, head propped

on one hand.

"She really is. It's nice to see her learn about livin' again," Ronny said, then added: "She smiles nice."

"She does."

"Do you think she'll stay?" Ronny asked.

"Course she'll stay. She needs us, don't she?"

Davey lay in bed and wondered about the question. He wondered if maybe they needed her more than she needed them. He closed his eyes and thought about apples and wishes and hoped that Miss Rose's wish—whatever it was—would come true anyway.

The boys fell asleep soon after the house sang its last song of settling boards, scurrying mice, and creaking stairs while the moon cast a spotlight on them, as if reminding God they were still there.

11

"I think we'll have Miss Rose tackle the chores by herself today," Maggie said.

"How's come?" Ronny asked.

"Sometimes it's best you let them figure it out on their own. Trial and error makes you smarter, makes you stronger here." Maggie tapped the side of her head.

"What about following by example? Doesn't that help, too?" Davey asked.

"Of course, dear. But nothing teaches you more than making mistakes. When there are consequences, then that's the best example to follow...of what not to do."

The boys seemed to ponder the lesson. Maggie patted the two on their heads and collected their empty plates.

"Can we have graham crackers and lemon pie tonight?" Ronny asked. "I like the crunch. And the pie tickles my tongue."

"You just like to spit the cracker dust," Davey said.

"That too. I pretend I'm a storm."

The two laughed and opened the books set in front of them: Two hardback copies of *The Complete Tales of Edgar Allan Poe* that smelled of mildew and dirt and time long used up.

The boys watched Miss Rose from their bedroom window while she weeded the flower garden below. She pinched each weed, pulled it from the root, and set them one by one into a metal pail by her side. Maggie had tied a strip of cloth around her head to keep the hair from her face and the sweat from her eyes. It covered the still-pink scar on her forehead and gave her a feminine appearance, like earrings or lipstick. Davey seemed to like that.

Then Miss Rose plucked a Jimson weed plant, smelled it and put it in her mouth, chewing it.

"No, Miss Rose. No!" Davey spoke to the bedroom glass.

"Is she fallin' back?" Ronny asked.

"Regressing? Nah. She's tryin' to taste. She's curious is all, but I don't want Miss Maggie seein' her like that, thinkin' she's no good."

"We should maybe tell her not to do that."

"Maybe." Davey agreed, but Ronny had gone back to playing with his guys as he called them, wooden figures Maggie had made especially for them. The boys had given each a name and with each name a super power. Then they'd painted them to reflect their powers. Bright orange for fire, blue for water, and black and purple for Owlman, the ruler of the night whose wings swept villains off their feet, crushing their spines against the desk and chair legs which acted as trees in a dense forest.

Davey looked once more at Miss Rose who'd gone back to weeding, then joined his brother in play.

"I read this thing once about this town in Europe, I don't think it was England. I think it was in Yugo...Yugosilva or somewhere. Anyway, one morning, might've been Christmas, the people woke up and found hoof prints in the snow all over the town."

Davey paused to gauge the level of interest his anecdote was receiving. Miss Rose was politely staring at him and Maggie at the counter rolling out the dough for yet another of her pies.

"So the weird part is the tracks were in twos, like someone on two legs made them. And they weren't tramped in the snow, they were melted into it. They went up and over rooftops and the sides of hills and all." Davey was talking fast now. He could not quell his excitement over all things strange and macabre.

"Where'd you read that tripe?" Miss Maggie asked, looking at him slyly, her left eye almost winked closed.

"A book by Charles Fort."

"*The Book of the Damned*?"

"Yeah, that was the name." His voice was a small thing then.

"From the bookshelf in my room?"

Davey hung his head and sheepishly glanced at Miss Rose, who feigned looking out the window.

"Yes, Ma'am."

"You know better, Davey. Those're my school books and all my teachin' and research books. Dryer than a popcorn fart and not of any interest to children. It's a bunch of old brittle words on brittle paper in there." She paused and softened her expression, "And Fort was a man given to folly and fraud."

"I'm sorry, Miss Maggie. I won't go in your room again." Davey slung his head so low his forehead nearly touched the wooden table top.

He felt old fingers on his shoulder and a grip that was hard but not angry. "Just ask me first next time, if you're after a particular subject. I'll let you know if I have anything to your liking. Ok?" Dry lips on his neck and a pat on the back, and then she was back to work on her pie. Davey looked at Miss Rose and she was smiling.

14

Like the day before, the boys were asked to keep away from Miss Rose. They were told she was still working the kinks out and it's best she was left alone. Reluctantly, the boys did just that. After their morning studies, they took to their own chores, sneaking peeks at Miss Rose as she washed the breakfast dishes, folded laundry from the line, and brushed cobwebs from the barn rafters. They watched with concern, wanting to help but trusting Maggie's words about what's best for the learning visitor.

For lunch, the boys were allowed to take their sandwiches and chips outside. They made their way to the barn's loft and sat on bales of hay, their backs resting on the old wooden beams, plates on laps.

"How about this one…'I became insane, with long intervals of horrible sanity,'" Davey said and then shoved a chip into his mouth.

"Lovecraft!" Ronny almost shouted.

"Close…and good guess, but that's wrong."

"Must be Poe. The insanity threw me, I think."

"Yup, Poe…how 'bout this one: 'Sometimes, the most profound of awakenings come wrapped in the quietest of moments.'"

"I can't remember that guy's name. I know he wrote the war book..." Ronny made an exaggerated "I'm thinking" face, complete with tip of the tongue sticking out over his lip.

"Close enough, Stephen Crane. You're thinking of *Red Badge of Courage*." Davey ate another chip and took a bite of his sandwich.

"My turn," Ronny said. "'In Heaven, everything is fine.'"

Davey thought long and hard about his answer and nearly guessed Bradbury. By default it was his favorite and the one Ronny most quoted during the game. Ronny watched his brother, grinning, waiting with a mouthful of honey-loaf and salty vinegar chips.

"Living or dead?" Davey asked.

"Hmmm…not sure."

"Give me a clue."

"It's a woman." Ronny swallowed the food and sipped from his soda.

"Mary Shelley?"

"Ehhhnt!" Ronny mocked the wrong-answer buzzer from a game show. "It's the girl in that black and white movie we saw with the guy who works at the factory and meets the girl, and they have the weird calf baby that makes the horrible noise. The lady lives in the heater thing."

"That's a movie. You can't do movies. It's gotta be books or authors. That's the rules."

"It's still a quote."

The hay behind them rustled in the corner. The boys turned to look. A cat crept slowly toward them, cautiously, its head bowed low.

"A cat!" Ronny yelled.

"Here, kitty, kitty." Davey tore off a piece of his

sandwich and stretched out his arm, offering the cat his food.

The cat's movement halted, skittish eyes back and forth between the boys, then it sat on hind legs and bathed its front paw. Davey tossed the bit of food toward the cat. It jumped back, then slinked forward, eyes on the food. It snatched the bit of sandwich and swallowed with barely a chew. It went back to looking at the boys, its eyes darting nervously.

"It's starving," Ronny said, tossing the cat the rest of his sandwich.

"She can be our pet maybe," Davey said.

"How do you know it's a girl?"

"Because it's pretty and white as snow with spots like freckles."

"Oh," Ronny said, not giving it another thought. "What can she eat? Besides our lunches, I mean. Do cats like mustard? What about corn?"

"Cats don't eat corn. We can give her the mice from the traps, maybe eggs from the hens. They like milk and fish."

"Boys?" A voice from below. It was Miss Rose. Her blouse was dirty, her red hair littered with bits of web and leaves. But her smile glowed. "How to get up there?"

The boys looked at one another, smiled. "We'll come down."

"You should see what we found, Miss Rose," Davey said as he climbed down the loft ladder.

"It's a kitty cat," Ronny blurted out, following his brother.

Davey jumped when there were still four rungs to

go. Ronny did the same. Miss Maggie didn't care for them being reckless. She'd tell them to be careful, always. Whether they were bailing hay, collecting eggs, or even doing the wash. She knew boys had a way of breaking unsuspecting bones and blackening eyes. She told them they were delicate and didn't understand their own fragility and that the world could swallow them up whenever it wants if they're not careful. And then what would she do?

"Where's the kitty?" Rose asked. She looked all around the open space of the barn.

"She needs to get used to us, I think…work things out. Like you, she'll be ready when she's ready." Ronny smiled, proudly.

Miss Rose tried to smile back but it was a broken thing that cowered away and went to her brow, where it furrowed and lay confused.

"Let's get you some tea," Davey said. "Miss Maggie makes the best mulberry black tea and left some on the counter for us before heading to town. All's we gotta do is put the kettle on. It'll do your bones some good." After Davey said it, he thought that last bit didn't make much sense, but it's what he learned so it's what he preached. One of many things.

"How you settling in?" Davey looked at Miss Rose when he asked it. He had read once that it was important to look a person in the eyes when they spoke. Words could bend or be outright hollow, but the eyes don't lie. She looked at the mug in her hands, at the dark liquid cooling in it. She glanced at Davey and smiled a half smile.

"Getting there." She brought the cup to her lips, the steam rose in front of her face like ghostly fingers.

"It takes time, for some," Davey offered and smiled.

"I remember things, but it's in pieces. And they don't always fit. Like one of them boxes with the little bits of hard paper in them. You put them together and make a picture..."

"A puzzle?"

"Yeah, a puzzle. Only my box doesn't have all the pieces. A lot of the pieces don't even seem to be from the same puzzle." Rose sipped her tea and tried on another smile, this one was too big.

"I know how that goes." Davey paused and lost himself in thought for a second before pulling himself back.

Ronny's voice could be heard outside as he played with his figures, marching them through the dangers of tall grass. Davey watched Miss Rose as she nursed her tea. "You want to hear a story? I can read pretty good and there's a whole bookshelf in the room there. Chores are all done. Miss Maggie's not back from town yet." Miss Rose nodded and her pale eyes almost closed.

"That'd be lovely. Sure." Her voice was a desiccated bee husk on a windowsill.

Davey went about finding a book and choosing a story that would make Miss Rose feel better, maybe happier. He found his hand nearing a collection by H.H. Munro when the screen door banged open and Ronny came rushing in, more mud than boy.

"It's coming down in buckets!" he shouted excitedly and then went about trying to wipe the mud from his legs but succeeded only in smearing it around more. Davey looked at him and shook his head, sighing as he did so. He looked to Miss Rose who was staring out the window and from the looks of it, out of this world altogether. She seemed hypnotized by the static lines and hiss of the sudden rain.

"Let's go get you cleaned up before Miss Maggie gets in and tans your hide for muddying up the place."

Ronny ran up the steps with slappy wet footprints, shedding soiled clothing along the way. "Can I use the bubbles?!" he hollered from above somewhere. Davey looked at Miss Rose once more and considered apologizing, but realized she wasn't even aware he was still in the room. His lips vanished and his head drooped as he made his way to the bathroom to take care of Ronny.

16

Miss Maggie sat in the cab of her battered old Chevy pick-up, fogged in cigarette smoke and looking somber. She had the driver's side window cracked and the smoke was filtering out in thin wisps. The steady drizzle pattered on the roof and sounded like someone shaking a tin can full of teeth. She stared at the small billboard across the road, not focusing on it enough to make out the words upon it. Her mind was on other things. She took the stub of a smoke from her lips and crushed it into the overflowing ashtray with the others. "That's just like my life." she muttered. A lot of promise and a few false starts, all of 'em stubbed to a smoldering demise at one point. She bowed her head into her hands and sat. The radio low but she could still faintly hear the Marty Robbins song wafting from the single working speaker.

She had gotten married right out of high school. Leonard had been the lucky one, courted her through senior year and kindly waited until she graduated to start with the stealthy anchors. The first was a ring and the second a baby in her belly. She was so thrilled, and thought he was too.

Until the night he came home drunk. The night he found her filling out paperwork to take classes at the local college. The night where the usual loud words graduated to open-handed smacks.

She never finished the paperwork and the classes

fluttered away. She stayed at the house all day, every day and cleaned and cooked and tried to be invisible. Len came home angrier and angrier, and the night she decided to say what was on her mind was the night he kicked their child out of existence. That next morning, when Maggie woke up tangled in bloody sheets and full of tears, Leonard climbed into his truck and drove off towards town. He was gone for two days before she realized he wasn't coming back.

Three months later, she started back to school. Five years after that she had her degree and a few more after that her doctorate. It was only after she settled into her after-study life that she recognized the empty spots it held...so many of them.

The horn blast shocked Maggie from her daze. She looked up in time to see the tail end of Horace Miller's wagon disappear around the bend. She looked at herself in the rearview. Red-rimmed eyes filled with anger and hurt. She sniffed and wiped the dregs of tears on her sleeve, then opened her window the whole way, indifferent to the slowing rain. She started the truck. It was time to get home and get on dinner.

***

Maggie pulled into the drive, her truck hopping on the graveled grooves, splashing through the puddles and gullies left by the shower. At one time, Leonard had promised a paved driveway but instead covered the worn trail in pebbles, most of which were long buried in the dirt. Two brown scars peppered with runaway stones that crackled under the weight of the truck.

The boys ran outside to help unload the feed and

37

groceries. Miss Rose stayed in, finishing off her tea, staring deep into the mug of brown liquid like her soul might be at the bottom.

17

The morning was hazy, as they often were in late summer. The air cool but it held humidity and fierce heat behind its back. Ronny was bent down, his hand extended toward the cat as it slowly made his way toward him.

"No sudden moves," Davey coached him.

The cat mewed and took the bread from his hand.

"I felt his whiskers. They tickle."

"Miss Maggie said they use them for balance."

The cat crept close to Ronny, rubbing against his leg.

"She likes you."

"Here," Ronny handed the rest of the bread to Davey. "You try."

Davey took a few steps forward, bent down and gave the cat the bread, which it gobbled down.

"Try petting her," Ronny said.

Davey stuck out his hand and the cat took to it, mashing its head up against his palm, walking under the press of his hand, its back arched high, then turning around for a repeat.

"She's purring," Davey said.

"Pick her up and let's go show Miss Maggie."

The cat dropped all guard and allowed the gentle squeeze of Davey's arms as they made their way to the house. Along the way, they ran into Miss Rose who was raking up hay that had blown out from the

39

barn during a recent storm, her penance for forgetting to pull the side door closed.

"We got the kitty!" Ronny beamed and pointed to the ball of fur in his brother's arms. Rose just nodded and went back to raking, her lips never stopped moving but neither boy could make out what she was saying.

"Miss Maggie!" Ronny hollered from the steps, they knew better than to take a critter across the threshold. Learned that lesson the day Davey caught the garter snake and surprised Maggie with it as she was peeling potatoes.

"What?! Has there been a murder!?" Maggie scurried out onto the porch all faux bug-eyed and shocked. She smiled and then laughed.

"We caught the kitty!" Ronny howled and petted the cat's tail. It squirmed in Davey's grip but didn't scratch or leap.

"We almost never get cats around here, for some reason. Not sure how you managed to get this one to sweeten up to you."

"I fed her pieces of bread until she came close and then picked her up."

"That so?" Maggie cocked her head and made like she didn't believe them, in actuality she was watching the woman over by the barn. The one raking without having the tines on the ground. The one whose eyes were rolled up white in her head. The one whose lips were moving like a preacher on Sunday morning when taken by the Spirit. Maggie took in Rose's state and never let it tarnish the plastic smile she had on for the boys.

"Well, put her down and then come in and get all the fur and dander offa ya, it's getting close to supper time."

"Can we keep her around?" Ronny asked.

Maggie eyed the cat, eyed the boys, then gave in.

"I don't see why not. Long as she keeps clear of the hens and makes herself useful on the barn mice."

"She's a fine hunter, I'm sure of it."

"I don't doubt that one bit." Maggie mussed Ronny's hair. "Now put her in the barn, then get yourselves cleaned up."

"Yes, Ma'am." The two replied, then headed to the barn.

18

Maggie retired early that evening. The day had worn her down, as the days seemed to do anymore, particularly during harvest. Maggie had even flirted with the idea of a hired hand to help with the tasks that had become too much for her, and certainly beyond the boy's threshold for labor.

That night, story time was skipped so Davey read aloud to Ronny and Miss Rose the tale he was most familiar with: Edgar Allan Poe's *The Black Cat*. Davey read slow, not because he had to but because he felt Miss Rose would better appreciate the story that way, maybe understand it better.

Miss Rose sat attentive, more than she'd ever had while at the farm. And it looked to the boys that she enjoyed every word. Miss Maggie would be pleased.

Toward the end of the story, Miss Rose spoke up. "May I read to you?"

The boys grinned wide and Davey happily handed over the book of stories. "Read this one," he said and opened to *The Tell Tale Heart.*

Miss Rose took the book in her lap and stared at the pages, the ink illustrations, flipping through them for quite some time before saying a word. "A man lived in a cabin. He...he took care of an old man with a glowing eye..."

It was clear right away that Miss Rose was not reading but using the illustrations to form a story of her own, and any attempt at reading tied her tongue and cast a frown upon her face. So the boys sat patiently as Miss Rose told her own story of a man taking care of a sleepless friend who never found comfort until napping in a special bed under the house. "Dirt is the closest thing to a womb that a person can hope for," she had said.

When Miss Rose finished the story, the boys quietly clapped and told her what a wonderful job she'd done. Her own smile was so big that teeth showed. It seemed that progress was certainly being made.

Ronny watched the cat through the screen door while he ate his oatmeal, packed with raisins. He liked how they turned the meal chewy. He'd once called the oatmeal boring and likened it to horse feed. Just going through the motion of spoonful after spoonful with nothing for your teeth to do. Monotonous was the word he was looking for that day, and Miss Maggie had schooled him on the word, which he never could remember. Too many syllables. So he learned to say tedious, and that was better.

"Won't be long 'fore Gentilbelle is in here, eating with us, bowl full of kitty food right there." Ronny nodded toward the floor next to him. "Wouldn't that be somethin'?"

"Sure would. And between you and me." Davey looked at Miss Rose, who poked at her oatmeal, sinking the raisins into the mush with her finger. "I think Miss Maggie is warming to her. I'll bet she'll let her in if we show we can take care of her and still stay on top of school and chores.'

"Are cats bad?" Miss Rose interrupted.

"What do you mean?" Davey asked.

"They will hurt you?"

"No way," Davey said. "Not Gentilbelle. She's a precious thing. Wouldn't hurt a fly."

"Her tongue feels like wet sand and tickles," Ronny offered.

"Cats can be snooty, sure. The Egyptians claimed them as gods, and at some point the cats started believin' it. Pretty stuck up critters. But I don't think they're evil."

"Okay, sorry." Miss Rose gave a look. There were traces of sadness and confusion in it.

"It's okay, Miss Rose. You're learning." Davey smiled at her.

"Davey, do you really think Miss Maggie will let Gentilbelle inside?"

"I do."

Ronny showed teeth with an oatmeal-covered grin and went back to watching the cat—that now lay in a patch of sunlight on the grass in front of the porch steps—and thought about life with a ball of orange and white fur curled on his pillow every night, purring in his ear, and decided he'd be the best cat owner there ever was.

Davey woke to Miss Rose standing over him. She was naked and the room smelled of feces. In her hand was Maggie's apron, and she was humming a song that sounded familiar but he couldn't place it. It stirred in him what felt like good memories, none of which he could place, like dreams long forgotten but the impression made still lingered.

"Miss Rose?"

"How is to put this on?" Miss Rose reached out, handing the apron to Davey. Her body shone like something carved from soap—bone white in the moonlight. She wore the same stitches as him, same as Ronny. Down her chest, between her breasts. Davey had never seen a woman in the nude. It stirred in him shame and embarrassment.

"W...where are your clothes?"

"I messed in them. Will you help me?"

"Umm...okay but…"

"What's goin' on?" Ronny stirred. His eyes widened at the sight of Miss Rose across the room.

"Cover your eyes, Ronny. You shouldn't be seeing Miss Rose like this."

"Neither should you!"

"She had an accident and come to me for help."

"You mean…?"

"Yes. Now go back to sleep 'fore Miss Maggie wakes up and catches you with an eyeful."

Ronny turned to face the wall and mumbled to himself as Davey slid from the bed and led the woman down the hall toward the bathroom. He slid his hand into the crook of her arm.

"What happened?" he whispered, more rhetorical than anything.

Miss Rose just made a soft whimpering noise. After they'd passed her darkened doorway, Maggie poked her head from the shadows and tilted it towards the door. She flared her nostrils and took in the stink. "Davey?" Her voice was a hammer on wood, abrupt and sturdy.

"We didn't mean to wake you Miss Maggie. Miss Rose had an accident." Davey couldn't steady his voice as he stood outside the bathroom door, holding the woman's arm as she held her head down and picked at the drying filth on her legs.

Maggie's brow furrowed and she frowned a bit, "Wait a minute and I'll take care of cleaning her up." She then slunk back into her room, like a beast to its cave, and returned just as quick. She tied the ratty striped robe around her and took Rose's hand from the boy.

"You go on to bed, son. You ought'nt be seeing a grown woman naked yet. Especially one in this sorry state."

Davey paused and looked at Rose, tried to make eye contact to let her know she was going to be okay. Rose just stared at the floor. Maggie looked Davey square on and said once more. "You just get back to bed."

As Davey opened the door to his room, he heard

the pipes clang as Maggie turned on the hot water. He heard her low voice muffled by door and wall. And then he only heard her singing.

21

Davey had been out on his own the morning he found Gentilbelle, her spine bent wrong and bloated with water in the barrel against the barn. He stared into it for what felt like hours before deciding Ronny couldn't see such a sight and would do his best to hide it. His little brother grew too attached to things that would up and leave, whether by death or just tired of life on the farm, and the boy often took it personal, like maybe he was the cause. This would crush him.

But while Davey stared into the barrel, his mouth hanging slack, thinking of what to do and why the world is such a damn cruel place, Ronny approached without warning.

"What is it?"

Davey started, slammed the lid onto the barrel and could only give a wordless look. It was an awful look. One Ronny had never seen his brother wear before. Not ever. It said that whatever was in that barrel was a terrifying secret, not for anybody's eyes.

"Davey, what's wrong?"

"You go on and clean up for lunch, Ronny. I'll be right behind you."

"No. You're hiding something. Something awful…I can tell."

There was no use arguing. Davey couldn't fake that what'd he'd just seen was anything less than

49

horrible, maybe even heartbreaking. Ronny prepared, then walked to the barrel and put his hand on the lid.

"You don't want to open that, Ronny. I'm telling you."

Ronny curled his lip as the smell inside crept out and met his nose. He'd smelled it plenty before. Sometimes the field mice would find their way in the walls during the winter, starve to death and send out a reek that'd last for weeks. Even a deer once wandered onto the land, hid among the tall grass and bled out from a hunter's shot. The odor brought them to it, and Maggie had the boys bury the thing beyond the tree line in a shallow grave that kept the reek at bay until the earth ate it up and spit out the bones.

"A 'coon?"

Davey's face was telling. This was no raccoon, no field mouse. This was family.

Ronny lifted the lid and put a hand to his mouth, catching the sad, weak breath that escaped as he laid eyes on their new pet. Gentilbelle floated in the barrel. Bulging, milky eyes shot a gaze at the space between the two boys, seeing nothing. The bloated body, unnaturally folded, bobbed in the water like a bean in soup, surrounded by loose hair and muddy film.

Ronny dropped the lid and ran for the house, his brother calling after him. The both of them in tears.

The screen door had barely banged shut before Miss Maggie turned from the stove to greet Ronny, his face red, wet with tears.

"Good morning, child."

"Miss Maggie." His voice evaporated near the end of her name.

"Yes." She stopped, wiped her hands on her waist apron and turned her full attention to him. He was upset and her heart leapt. "What is it?"

Ronny went to her, threw his arms around her waist and muffled his sobs against her stomach. He told her about the horrible thing they'd found. Maggie smoothed his hair down and held him tight until he calmed and then told him she was sorry, that Gentilbelle was a good cat which didn't deserve such an end. That the pet dearly loved him and was lucky to be his and that those few days were no doubt the best of its life.

"How could such a thing happen?"

"I don't know, dear. I just don't know." She said this as her eyes fell on the woman outside picking at the grass by the porch, mistaking flowers for weeds. The woman with the fresh scratches on her arm.

The sky was a bruised eyelid, purple brown until the heat lightning flashed. Maggie sat in her rocker on the porch, the screen door behind her propped open with an old cinder block. "Night breeze is the best air freshener there is" she'd say as she sat on the porch like a gargoyle with an ever-present Marlboro. She stubbed out her smoke in the upturned box turtle shell she kept on the crate beside her. She closed her eyes and inhaled the evening. Damp grass and lightning bugs. Moist earth and pollen. She was just starting to smile when the footsteps behind her broke the mood. Miss Rose sat down on the swing across from her.

"Evening, doll," Maggie said, her teeth showing in a smile that was less than genuine.

"Evening." Rose looked out at the tree line and the pin points of yellow light that bobbed as the fireflies did their thing. She gasped and looked to the old woman in the chair, "Are those faeries?"

Maggie slightly sneered as smoke rolled up over her face and into the dusk. "Lightning bugs."

"Quite pretty," was all Rose said.

"I was just meanin' to come inside and get you." Maggie fished another cigarette from the box on the chair arm and then held it out to Rose, who shook her head, never taking her eyes off the crone. "Knew you was smart." She paused again to kiss the tip with a lighter flame and draw in a billow of carcinogenic smoke.

"Did you need me?" Rose asked.

"Funny thing. I thought that I did. But it seems I was mistaken." Maggie smoked and stared at the other woman, who seemed to be growing more uneasy with every silent second that eeked by. Abruptly, Maggie stood and took the younger woman's hand in her own, ran a bony finger along the bright red wounds on her arm. Crimson lightning in an ivory sky. "Let's go out to the barn, I have a present for you."

Rose smiled and looked down at the shorter woman. "You didn't have to go and do that."

Maggie smiled and winked an eye in the fluorescent light of the pole lamp, "Now, honey, that's where you'd be wrong."

Maggie pulled open the barn door and they went inside.

24

"I can't find Miss Rose." Ronny spoke in that halting way of his. He stood in the doorway with his shoes on, the stain of grape juice circling his lips.

Davey put the boxes from breakfast back in the cupboard, then turned to his brother.

"I'll help you look as soon as I ready up from breakfast." He put the cap back on the milk and stuck it in the fridge. Ronny watched him impatiently.

"What do you want her for?"

"To tell her about Gentilbelle and see if she wanted to play in the dirt pile with my men."

"I doubt she'd want to do that." Davey spoke with certainty.

"I bet she would. She's a nice lady."

"I haven't seen her. Might be she's sick again and took to her bed. Maybe sleepin'."

"She's not in her room. I looked." Ronny could be obnoxious when petulant.

"Come on. I'll play with you."

Ronny gave a weak smile, doing his best to not think of bloated Gentilbelle. "I've got the rubber bands." Then he rushed through the screen door, Davey following behind.

The two sat at the foot of the pile of soil beside the tractor shed, positioning a battalion of plastic figures on palm-flattened ridges and in finger-carved caves. The quiet farm filled with mouthed explosions and bursts of victory as the rubber band artillery exploded dirt and picked off the still soldiers one by one.

Davey looked up to the house and saw Maggie standing at the screen door, watching them. She turned and faded away. The bad feeling growing in Davey's stomach did not.

"I'm sorry you boys are sad that Miss Rose left us, but I don't have no answers for you." Maggie spoke quickly, in between heaving breaths as she stood on the compost heap, stabbing it with a pitchfork. Once a week she did this, turning it to allow the fresher material to breakdown and decompose within the internal oven of the mound. Her black rubber boots glistened with the slime of the rotting rinds and cores. Flies buzzed and dove like kamikazes. She never raised a hand to them.

"Why you think she did it?" Davey stood with his hip cocked and his hand over his eyes to shield the morning sun's glare from them.

"One never knows, Son. Some people have wings on their heels and others feet of lead. Some have anchors and others have threads that attach to whims and pull them along. I guess our Rose was one with wings and threads."

She forked a pile of putrid lettuce and egg shell to the side and then pulled out a hole in the mound to push it into. Steam rose around Maggie like a ghoul from a Hammer film. The air was thick and sour. Davey said nothing, just nodded and turned to head to the house.

Maggie looked down and saw the arm jutting from the back of the heap. Brown grime obscuring the ivory skin, freckles dotting it. Sometimes coons or possums dug where they shouldn't, uncovering secrets and threatening to taint the life on the farm Maggie had worked so hard to create.

She looked back to Davey who was ascending the hill now, and forked some refuse over the limb. She spit and turned the compost.

The boys stood behind the barn and stared at the etched tree carved into the aging wood. It was a crudely rendered tree, but that's what it was. Davey couldn't remember how long ago he carved it into the barn, but he never forgot the first blood print. It was painful, emotionally and physically. He had sliced his thumb open with a small pocket knife and bled, then dotted his finger and pressed it against the barn. A blood apple on a chicken-scratch tree limb. Symbolism that Ronny didn't understand until Davey spelled it out.

"What're you doing?" Ronny had asked as he stood behind the barn, watching Davey work his knife against the wood. He whisper-counted the rust-colored smudges on the limbs while waiting for an answer. Davey kept silent, then cut his thumb while Ronny went wide-eyed. He then dipped a finger in red and pressed it against the barn.

"There…that's Sam." Davey finally said, wiping his thumb on his shorts. Ronny stepped closer and scrutinized the drawing. A simple tree, gouged into wood, three old fingerprints the color of fallen leaves, then the fresh one near a bottom branch. Sam.

"What is this?" Ronny's mouth agape, fish eyes filled with wonder.

"Our family tree." Davey smiled and pointed to the bloody swirls that marred it. "That's Rick. Remember Rick? And that one is old Milford. I didn't really like

him...always wanted me to sit on his lap."

"What are the two branches at the top, the ones without fruit?" Ronny seemed to be unable to generate enough spit to properly wet his throat. "That's your branch and Miss Maggie's. I love you best so you're at the top."

Ronny smiled, and with wet eyes walked over to Davey. He threw his short arms around him and squeezed. Davey leaned down and into it, embracing him back.

"I love you best, too. And I'm never leaving," Ronny whispered into Davey's chest.

And now Ronny gulped hard with anticipation. It was his turn to add to the tree. Stalling, Ronny said, "What if she comes back?" But he knew better. They never came back.

"Do you want me to do it?" Davey asked.

"No. I'll do it." He puffed his chest, the stitches under his shirt pulling tight. The sinew from a crow's foot.

Ronny took the knife from Davey and pulled the blade across his thumb. The metal split skin but no blood came.

"Deeper."

Ronny grimaced and retraced the superficial opening, pushing harder. Crimson wet the blade. "Here's to your wish coming true, Miss Rose. You were somethin' special." Ronny added a print to the family tree, then felt like crying. So he did.

27

Summer was sliding away, like carrion from bone. The boys were quiet these days, still marred by the disappearance of Miss Rose and the death of Gentilbelle. Maggie wore deeper worry lines than usual. Autumn would be knocking soon enough, and there was plenty of end-of-season work ahead of them, now down a pair of hands. The little bit of livestock needed tending and set for winter, the crops wouldn't harvest themselves—not to mention the tiresome rituals of plastic over windows, closing off the drafty rooms on the second floor. All things that came easier with the use of an extra set of hands, particularly with Maggie gradually slowing down. Creaking joints and blackened lungs.

"Soon summer will be over." Ronny spoke, and his voice was like a pinch in the quiet of the morning. Davey sat on the lower step and stared at the mist rising from the grass, reminding him of stories he'd read, of phantoms rising homeward.

"There'll be other summers. Winters too. Time just keeps coiling around, Ronny. It's what it does." He paused and bit his top lip a little, "Actually, that's *all* it does."

"Do you think Miss Maggie will bring someone else? Somebody to help with the fall stuff?" Ronny tilted his head with the question, as he always did.

"I don't know, I'd reckon she might. But you never

can tell what she may or may not do." Davey looked to the spot by the barn where Maggie's truck rested between journeys. Empty now, it was just a patch of crushed gravel with oil-stained spots and patches of dead grass like doll's hair crushed under the weight of the truck, under the weight of summer. Davey felt a strange envy for those patches. He sat up straighter and looked to his brother.

"Well, I don't know about any of that but I know we have a sunny nice morning and our chores all caught up, and we'd be fool to sit here and waste it moping about. Besides..." He jumped up and playfully slapped the younger boy on the back and waited for him to react.

"Besides what?" Ronny looked surprised, and a little upset at being hit.

"You're it." Davey hollered and took off in a sprint towards the lower yard. Ronny smiled and ran after, not a hope in hell of catching up to the taller, faster boy. They ran through the yard and through the field, pretending all was normal. That everything was fine.

Summer was sliding away, like carrion from bone.

28

A man sits at the bar on the corner of 28th and Harvard. In happier days he went there with friends, to tie one on, maybe shoot some pool and leave with a smile and an evening full of memories. Ten years later he's there to forget. The laughter around him penetrates nothing. He's a wart on a stool, a silent bummer and nothing else. The world moves on around him.

The clock-light on the wall that always declares *It's Miller Time* pretends its second hand still exists, as the long hands shift toward the next hour in slow, parkinsonian rhythm. The damn thing has been there from day one. Pretending, just like he does.

"One more, Lou," the barkeep says. He owns the bar, *Mac's Place*, and has for the better part of twenty years. He was there when Lou met his wife, right there in the corner booth. And he was there the night he lost her.

"I'm good." Lou pushed the rest of his drink away. He had a limit. While he used the bottle to escape, he didn't hate himself enough to make work the next day that much harder. He learned in that first month after Carol's death he couldn't hold a job without that limit, and surprised himself he even cared. But work was the only thing that seemed to keep him sane anymore. That and the booze from the smoke-filled bar that seemed to give him the best and worst in life, dangling the most beautiful thing he'd ever seen in front of them, then snatched it away soon after she was his.

Lou rubbed at the tattooed "C" on his ring finger. He'd gotten it after she passed and now it seemed like a bad idea. It was supposed to be a tribute to his late wife, something he'd glance at now and then and remember good times. But it was nothing but a constant reminder that she was gone. A child between them would have been ideal. A living, breathing thing that held her eyes, her dimpled smile. Any damn thing. And they had tried, but life shit on that, too. He rubbed harder at the tattoo. Yeah, maybe a bad idea.

Mac took Lou's glass and emptied it, wiped the bar clean, and pulled the till, started counting it. Lou was the last one out. He left so Mac could count in peace. Nobody likes that kind of cloud around them, not for that long. Lou said goodnight and walked out the door.

Lou's house was two blocks away. He didn't get a place so close to Mac's on purpose. It just happened that way, just like Carol's diagnosis. Shit just happens.

Lou made it a block down the street before stopping at a bench to sit. It was 2:00 a.m. The street was empty of all but cars tucked in for the night along the road. He breathed a deep breath full of grief and whiskey. The sky above was a sea of motor oil and diamond buckshot, the air smokestack ejaculate and lingering diesel.

A truck pulled up and stalled in front of him, an

older woman behind the wheel. She popped the hood and exited the truck, walked to the front, lifted the hood and tinkered with the engine. Her movements were mechanical, familiar. She'd done this before. She got back in the truck and turned the key. Nothing. Back to the engine for more tinkering.

"Like me to take a look?" Lou asked.

"If you don't mind. She gives out on me from time to time. Can't say I'm not used to it. If you could keep the carb open while I turn her over I think she'll start."

Lou got under the hood, opened the valve on the carburetor with his finger. "I'm no mechanic, but it may do you good to keep some carb cleaner in the truck...hell, even a stick to prop the valve if it happens often enough."

"I find this works best," the woman said, then raised a hammer and brought it down on the back of Lou's head.

29

They always came at night. The new ones. Maggie never had any other reason to be driving after dark, not this late. She'd be the first to proclaim her eyes weren't what they used to be even in broad daylight. Per routine, the boys watched again from their window. It was bittersweet. Too much loss that summer. Miss Rose, like Ronny had said, was something special. And the cat? That was a dream come true, one that ended prematurely, traumatically so. It was a deep scar that kept Ronny up at night, petting his pillow as though the dream never died.

The slow grind of gravel under Maggie's truck sounded like false hope. Like endless beginnings and beginnings of ends. Those tires a teasing crunch that always led to heartache.

The boys sat in silence as Maggie unloaded the truck. She couldn't carry this one. This time they were rolled from the truck bed, then dragged through the barn doors over the wide crack of rafter lights that splashed onto dirt like too much spilled milk.

"He's a big one," is all that was said. Then they lie on their backs, eyes to the ceiling, minds on just how tired they were. Tired of hurting. Tired of loss. The moon hung in the mid-September sky and stood sentinel.

30

Trying to lift the boy's spirits, just before bed Maggie read from *Dandelion Wine*. Their minds were elsewhere, not on Green Town or Cream-Sponge Para Litefoot Shoes, but on the large man brought home the night before and how long before it was Davey's turn to split his thumb and mark the tree.

Maggie sensed their grief, as well as the growing wall between her and the boys.

"Who is up for ice cream? The cold flesh of ice giants to tickle the brain?"

The boys said nothing.

"Sprinkled with squirrel bones, covered in the darkest of faerie blood?"

Two struggling smiles formed, and Maggie was off to fill three bowls filled with vanilla ice cream, crushed nuts, and chocolate syrup, all while singing a song she'd taught them years ago, hoping they would join in. They did, but they were broken voices that spilled like sap from a dying tree.

While eating, the sound of spoons clinking bowls bounced through the empty house, until each boy was done and retired to bed after weak hugs and the wishing of pleasant dreams that would probably never come.

Maggie smoked more than her usual share on the porch that night, damning the man in the barn to hell if he didn't go above and beyond. And by God leave the barnyard critters alone should one want to friend her boys. And to hell with him if he couldn't father these boys like they needed. Because she decided right then under the moon and its glow that maybe it's what they needed all along. A father.

31

At the table during breakfast, the boys took note right away of the man's strength. And cognitively he was beyond expectations, particularly for a new arrival. So far.

"Pass the honey, if you don't mind, Miss Maggie," Benjamin said.

Maggie, with a smile she had barely been able to shed all morning, happily passed the honey and winked at the boys, who watched the man inquisitively—with optimism even, despite the desire to guard their hearts. Benjamin seemed different.

The man rubbed at the back of his head while eating his cereal, wincing when he pushed too hard.

"You look awful brawny. How are you at lifting?" Ronny asked.

Benjamin stopped chewing and his brow furrowed, searching for an answer to give the boy. "I think I might be pretty good at it, young man." He then stuck his arm under Ronny's chair and lifted it inches off the ground. Ronny teetered in his chair, holding tight to his seat. The man's lip curled into something that was trying to be a smile, his eyes rolled, and a mumbling of nonsensical words came out. The chair dropped and the man winced once more at the pain in his head. Ronny nearly bit his tongue on landing and let out a nervous laugh.

"I think you might be the strongest man I ever

seen, Mr. Benjamin," Davey said.

"Give him a minute, boys. He might seem fine but he's already exerting himself. That's no good these first few days. Mr. Benjamin, you best go lie down.

Benjamin stood slowly, stared at the table, at the boys, at Miss Maggie, trying to make sense of it all it seemed. Then made another effort at that smile, as though trying to be polite even though it may physically hurt like hell to do so. He then turned and walked to the corner of the kitchen where he stood with his face toward the cupboards like a child in trouble. He stood that way until Maggie rose and laid a small hand on his arm and led him down the hallway and to his room.

32

"C'mon now, Mr. Benjamin. Eat your dinner. Them boys is waitin' to take you outside," crowed the woman from the kitchen.

Benjamin sat and stared at his plate. The pile of white fluffy, what had she said they were?...*mashed potatoes*. He poked them with a hesitant fork and touched them to his tongue. No taste. He dropped the utensil and looked at the small green pellets and the thin slabs of brown stuff, "Roast," he reminded himself. That was what the rosy-cheeked woman had said it was, "And lima beans." None of it had any taste at all.

He looked over at the boys. They both sat, watching him. The taller one leaned over to the small one, his dark bangs hanging in his clear blue eyes. "I think he's getting it," he whispered.

Ronny stole a nervous glance at the kitchen and smiled at the bigger boy. "I think so, too."

Davey listened to the off-key singing, the sound of running water and tinkling silverware. Miss Maggie was doing the dishes. His mind was reeling with a sense of deja vu at the whole scene, his eyes fixed on the man with not much of a memory staring at his cold plate.

The woman came in from the kitchen and picked up the almost untouched food. "Guess someone isn't hungry." She leaned a little and kissed the man's forehead. The lump was about gone, just the little kiss of scab remained. The spot where he fell face first into the truck's engine. She smiled at the boys; it was a very warm smile. "Go on outside, you lot. Maybe Benjamin will join you tomorrow. I'll tidy up the dishes and then we'll make a cake after it gets dark. Sound fun?" She stood with her hands on her hips.

"Yes, Ma'am" they answered and scampered from the table. Benjamin remained seated for a minute before pushing away and standing. The popping of his spine sounded like tap shoes.

33

Benjamin left his bedroom and made his way down the hall and toward the kitchen table, his boots heavy as cement. His head was foggy and he couldn't place things. Names of objects. He was a newborn calf, gangly and awkward. The smaller boy met him in the hall and held onto one of his hands; Ronny, he had heard the woman call him. Benjamin looked down at the boy and smiled. The boy looked anxious until they made their way through the kitchen and onto the porch, where they carefully took the steps one by one. The sun was on its way to setting, and the sagging barn cast a long, crooked shadow where they stood.

"Hurry up, Davey!" Ronny shouted. He let go of Benjamin's hand and looked up at the man's face. So many little lines, like a nervous sketch artist had drawn his features. Lines nested at the corner of his bleary eyes, beside his nostrils. His sallow cheeks were sprouting a carpet of grey and brown stubble. The scab above his right eye was a small red dot. Ronny stood on tiptoes and did his best to look Benjamin in the eyes, still an inch shy of the man's chin. "We'll set you straight in a minute, when Davey gets his ass out here." And with that the screen door banged open and the taller child bounded down the steps. He had put on a sweatshirt and held another one in his hands.

"Here, it's kinda chilly in the evenings now," he said, thrusting the extra into the smaller boy's arms. Davey and Ronny each took one of the man's hands and walked around the barn.

They reached the pasture past the barn where a circle had been flattened in the tall grass. A spot for summer-day lunches and army men games. Ronny sat and patted the ground next to him, never letting go of the man's hand. "Sit next to me, Mr. Benjamin."

Benjamin bent one knee, then the other before dropping to the grass and crossing his legs, watching the sun dip into the earth, either with fascination or an insecurity that he'd ever see it again. He held his hand up over his eyes and gave a crippled smile that probably felt better than it looked.

"It's beautiful," he said.

The boys looked across the field, each blade of grass frosted orange at the tip.

"You comin' out of it a little, ain't ya, Mister?" Davey asked in a hushed tone.

"Might be," he mumbled. Words were hard it seemed. They took their time coming out as he plucked the letters from a foggy mind, stringing them together in a sensible fashion.

"It's okay. It comes quicker for some than for others."

"Come out of what?" The man assembled words with the speed of a slug.

"The Waking up part," Davey replied as though it made perfect sense.

"I see."

"We've had folks who never came out of it, or

never got it right when they tried."

"What happened to them?" The man's voice was cave deep.

"They just weren't here anymore. Here one day, gone the next. Maggie says they rambled on."

Ben nodded and winced at the discomfort the action seemed to cause.

Davey looked down at Ben's hands. They were tired from work, deep grooves set into his knuckles where dirt stained the skin there.

"What's that mark there on your finger?"

Ben looked down and rubbed at it. "Not sure. Just a part of me, I guess." Then Ben turned back to watching the sun and its slow crawl behind the pasture.

Davey sighed and stood up from the grass. "Let's go back in. We can talk more another day, when some of the rust has come off."

"We'll be the oil, Mr. Benjamin." Ronny smiled.

"Will that be long?" Benjamin asked.

"Not fair to say. But if you ask me, I say you're a quick one. I can tell."

"I dunno. I don't think I was ever what you'd call...quick witted...nor quick on the draw." Ben smiled, and painful as it was, it was important he let them see he'd made a joke. The three made their way back to the house, Benjamin turning back often to gaze at the sun.

Ronny held the man's hand and didn't let go until they were inside.

Benjamin was downright keen of story time, though he took more to the stories with hope and love and dreams fulfilled, and found Poe, Lovecraft, and any mention of losing one's mind or paranoid delusions troublesome and one night even called them unhealthy. Said they tainted a bright soul. The boys chalked his words up to being nonsensical, more gibberish he was still working through. But through those story times the three bonded, and Miss Maggie all but retired from the nightly ritual, as Benjamin, it turned out, was a quick learner when it came to the written word and so cherished his time as the storyteller, reading aloud uplifting tales with charismatic narration that impressed Miss Maggie and the boys alike.

Benjamin found a real passion in books, and when chores were done and the boys were not in want of a third party for play, Benjamin could be found devouring page after page in the comfort of a living room chair or hidden away in his room, lost in "healthy" tales that he attributed to his progressive learning, the likes of which the household had never seen. Benjamin brought hope and love back to Maggie's farm.

September was worn down to the ribs, tired and wheezing as it did its best to hold on for another two weeks. From behind the barn, voices rose on the breeze like birds. One of those voices steadier than it was only a week before, when it was trudging through mud trying to find words that made any sense.

"Okay, Benjamin. I'm tired of goin' through this and losin' folks I come to like." Davey frowned when he spoke.

"Maybe you could call me Ben." The man said quietly, then paused, "It's easier."

"Ronny and I been here a long time. And we've seen people come and go. Usually just when we're gettin' used to them being around. We don't wanna see you up and leave us one day before you got your bearings, or maybe not being needed at all 'cause Miss Maggie thinks you'll never be ripe enough, so we wanna help you however we can."

"Ain't I doin' good?"

Davey let out a sigh. "You are, Ben. And that's what scares me. You up and leave us, I don't think Ronny'd ever come back to his right self. While there are things amiss here, things I don't quite understand and maybe shouldn't question, you being who you are, being the best visitor this farm has ever seen...Well, you're a treasure, Mr. Benjamin. A well-needed one."

Ben gave a gentle smile, then nodded and tilted his head towards the house. "It's different here. She takes good care of you boys, me as well. But underneath that there's something not right." Ben stole another look to the house, at the screen door to make sure the old woman wasn't watching. "I been reading."

"I know you do. You read books like I ain't ever seen. Like they was food." Davey smiled broadly.

"I've been reading *her* books," Ben clarified, and the smile blew from Davey's face like a cloud.

"She won't like that." Davey spoke barely above a whisper.

"I'm careful, don't worry. Between her books and journals, I think I sussed a few things."

Ben was about to lean in and offer up his new knowledge when the screen door banged and the crone appeared on the porch.

"Fellas! Soup's on!"

Ben and Davey stood and there was an awkward silence and something frightening in the air, and Davey wasn't sure he wanted to know what Ben had to say. He had questions, had them for a while now. But getting the answers scared him more than anything.

The two started toward the house and made near to the porch before Ronny came barreling around from behind the barn, "Oh boy! I like soup...long as they got chestnuts in it." His chipper voice was like a drop of oil in water against the somber air Davey brought with him.

77

36

It was several days later before Ben got the chance to get the boy alone and finish their chat. They found their way out behind the barn, something of a secret place now, what with the tree etching and now the taboo conversations.

"Okay. I'm just gonna spill it. For starters. I think we're dead. I am, so is Ronny and you are too." Not a flicker of a smile or anything to betray it as a sick joke. Ben's face was cemetery stone, and he watched as Davey made his eyebrow arch. "I know…listen I know I've not been here that long. I mean, long enough but not as long as you fellas. An' I know you said there been a few who ain't here no more. Miss Maggie, I'm thinkin' she's like a witch. Kinda. Maybe not even. I don't understand what she does or how she makes it work. I know she has books. Dozens of 'em, maybe hundreds. I looked at some…read them a bit, and I know she got some up in the extra room about tribes on them islands. And how they bring back the dead. She maybe got the how from them. She's a real smart lady. She's nice enough. I sorta like her. And I definitely feel sorry for her." Ben stopped speaking, his speech in almost frantic spurts, and Davey just stared at him. His face told Ben he was putting pieces together, that questions were being answered. And the answers hurt. They hurt real bad.

"I think I've known some of this for a long time."

Davey spoke the words very calmly.

A crow cawed from the rafters inside the barn and the boy quieted. After a few weighted moments, Davey continued. "She never had a family, though I think she might have had a husband back in younger years. I think. She may have mentioned him in a bitter way. But no kids. I just always been here. She's lonely, Maggie is. But she says I'm her firstborn. I can't remember much of anything before my thirteenth birthday, maybe twelfth. I only recall that on account of Maggie baking me a big chocolate cake. Ronny ate up most of the icing before we even got to cutting it, then said he didn't do it, all the while covered in brown, looking like a pig fresh from the mud pit. It's funny how I got so much I can't remember and then big slabs of things I can. I been here since. That was years ago. Maybe like ten? Maybe only four? Time moves fast, or not at all anymore." Davey paused and bit his lip as Ronny came bounding around the barn, one of his toy men gripped in his hand.

"Hi, guys!" he hollered before Ben held up a finger and nodded to Davey to let his brother know there was serious talk going on. Ronny dropped to the ground and crossed his legs. "Sorry," he said.

Davey cleared his throat and went on speaking. "I remember that she told me once of how she saw me at a carnival and knew I was her boy. She followed me and told me she had a puppy in her truck an' asked did I wanna see it. I musta said sure an' that was that, she took me away."

Davey stopped talking as he noticed Ronny's lip

quivering and tears welling in the boy's eyes. "Cover your ears, Ronny. I know this part upsets ya." His pudgy hands flew up and covered his ears. He began to hum his song about the geese and ducks.

"So you've known about what she does all this time?" Ben was incredulous but also somehow moved by the boy's loyalty in light of the circumstances.

"I suppose we have," was all Davey could offer back.

"She killed me, like she killed him and like she killed you. And all them ones who are gone. She's got to. If we're to be her family, she's gotta kill us to erase what we was. Then she'll bring us back for her. We're like jars that have to be emptied and cleaned out before she can fill us with what she wants us to know." Ben was standing now and pacing a little as he rambled.

"She told me she waited until I was asleep, put a pillow over my face until I was still. Then she did the magic thing. I don't know what that is, she never says so, then I woke up. I was back again. I don't know nothing much about before. But she takes care of us. Feeds us, even though ya can't taste nothin' no more."

Davey looked at Ronny who still had his hands over his ears and tapped his shoulder. "I'm done with that part now." Ronny smiled and took his hands down. "I was singing that song about the ducks and gooses in my head."

"You must have a hole in your head, 'cause we could hear you singing it loud and clear right here," Ben said with a serious face, causing Ronny to look absolutely shocked. They all laughed a bit, then Ben roped them back to the topic at hand.

"How do you know this, if she..." Ben looks at the younger boy and then back to Davey. "Does that to ya to empty your head? How'd you know all this other stuff then?" Ben asked, frowning. Not an angry frown, a confused one. It seemed to take an eternity to put that question together. Overhead, bats fluttered from the eaves of the barn.

"I don't rightly know, I guess after so long little bits of memories are bound to swim up from deep down. Maybe she's getting old and her magic getting sloppy. Maybe she talks to me when I'm sleepin' and tells me stuff outta loneliness or guilt. You read the stuff in her books. I ain't sure. I just know it's the truth, or feels just like it." Davey looked almost offended at Ben's questions.

They heard the dragonfly drone of a truck engine in the distance. Davey stood and walked back to where he had dropped the rake he was using to drag out old vine from the lattice along the side of the house. Ben stood and picked up Ronny and held him on his hip. The boy smiled and hugged the man tightly.

"I don't like that sort of talk," the little boy said in his ear. Ben said nothing, just hugged him back as he walked around to the front of the barn and watched as Maggie drove up the lane.

81

37

They sat in the shade of the apple tree, having just explained the wish game to Ben. He had managed to twist the stem three times before it broke, then made a wish. Somehow this brought a melancholy air to the game as Davey recalled Miss Rose's attempt at a wish.

After a few minutes, Ben asked "Why don't you run away?"

"We can't. Look here," Davey said. The boys took Ben by the hands and led him to the fence line. Little Ronny looked up at the haggard man and smiled, "She's a nice lady, Mister Benjamin. She sings to me at bedtime, she makes cakes and pies and the best cookies I ever did eat!" His little round face seemingly cherubic in the light of a dying sun.

"But you can't even taste them, son."

The smile that was planted on Ronny's face left quick like as he pretended the words weren't true.

They stopped walking and Davey gestured towards the fence row. Thick wooden posts strung with thin grey wire held the frayed ribbons of cloth every five feet or so. Red flannel strips and cotton swatches. Shreds of green material and billowing streamers of yellow fabric dotted the fence line. The three walked to the end of the fence row, where the lane meets the paved road and the mailbox stands. Tied around the mailbox post was a garland of denim and corduroy. A sun-faded trucker hat that may have been blue once bobbed in the light breeze from the cloth strip that tethered it there. They looked up and saw the power line that runs from the corner beam of the barn all the way down the road, littered with strips of multicolored material.

Where the power line veered into the woods that border the property, they saw the trees were marked with more cloth, more denim squares. A few of the skinnier saplings had socks tied around their thin trunks.

Ben looked confused until Davey explained: "That's our fence. A real fence is nothing to us, so she went and built us one from scraps of our clothes and the clothes of the ones that aren't with us anymore. Dead can't cross the dead, I think is the thing she said. Which didn't mean a thing to me until you told me of your findings. It's like I knew, but I didn't. Something in me did but left well enough alone. This line here, this is like a force field from one of them space movies."

Ben shook his head. Ronny slipped his small hand into the man's larger, shaking one. They stood there staring at the dangling makeshift ribbons for a long time. The sun slid behind the mountain and surrendered to blossoming darkness.

The man looked down and managed a weak smile. "I guess we're a family now. Seems sort of like I'm the Pa."

The boys looked at him and their eyes grew wetly bright. "Sort of," the youngest child spoke, and they began the walk back to the farmhouse while Ronny sang about the muffin man.

38

The summer continued to wither and fade into autumn. Ben and the boys had several more secret chats behind the barn. The most recent between Davey and Ben, only as they sensed a reluctance from young Ronny when the subject turned to the more morbid details of their existence.

"Ya know, I read this book of hers about voodoo, not the islandy kind. This was concernin' mountain folks. Appalachians, they was called. I think down south maybe. Coulda been anywhere, them mountains stretch forever. The book was about stuff like folk religions. I remember bits of text but it's all jumbled up. Anyway, in a lot of these things, they can bring the dead to life again, and they have all sortsa ways they do it. But they all had one thing in common. The person what raised the dead had to excise the heart."

"What's excise mean?"

"Remove. They remove the heart."

Davey felt through his shirt at the ribbed sutures that had been there an eternity.

"They cut them out and keep them, along with something of theirs from when they was alive. This becomes like an anchor to the dead. It's also how they worked them, like a puppet with no strings. Then they hide it so nobody could take the power back." Ben shook his head as he recalled this.

Davey just sat on a hay bale, his head in his hands. "What're you thinkin' about this for, Ben?" he asked after a minute. Ronny sat by the far door, singing to a row of wooden toy men he had leaned against the barn.

"I'm thinking this ain't right. She's a nice lady and she ain't hurtin' us or really no one else. Not now, anyway. But what if we had families before? I mean, you did, I may have. What about Ronny? He's a good little boy. She didn't have no right to steal someone else's family and make 'em hers. And on top of that, she killed us. We're supposed to be dead, Davey. Even if it was murderous dead, dead is what we're meant to be." Ben got more agitated. "Don't you feel a buzz in ya?"

Davey felt a blossom of unease uncoiling in his chest. He thought hard about Ben's words. They felt like poison. He thought of Ronny, about how him maybe having another brother out there. A real brother. Maybe a sister. A mother and father.

"A buzz?"

Ben looked around to make sure no one was listening. "I gotta buzz in me, all the time. Like I'm fulla hornets. It burns in my chest and hums in my ears and it sure ain't restful. I think it's because we're meant to be dead. It's our lot. We gotta find our hearts and be as we was meant to. I like you boys. Hell, you're like sons to me after these long weeks, but we belong in a better place."

Davey said nothing, just stood and slowly walked toward the house, leaving Ben to sit in the growing shadows as the sun faded. Ronny kept singing to his guys.

39

Davey broke from trimming the bushes on the side of the house to wipe the sweat from his brow. The hot days weren't over yet but grew fewer, with the occasional one making the idea of cooler weather more attractive as time went on.

Ronny pulled clothes from the line and dumped them in a basket. Maggie would just as soon not have him fold them, as his tiny hands couldn't quite manipulate the clothes like hers could.

Ben, in a stride that tried to hide any urgency to it but failing, made his way to Davey.

"Davey, I found them."

"Found what?"

"In the barn, a false wall behind a stack of hay, like a closet where there shouldn't be. They was in there."

"What was?"

"It's best I just show you." The two walked to the barn where Ben led Davey to the back, then pulled down a stack of hay and tugged at a loose board behind them. The board came loose, then dropped, as did Davey's jaw.

Across a thick plank inside the wall were several small objects spaced evenly apart that upon first glance resembled apples that'd seen too much sun, all held in place by long nails. Above each was a small fat candle melted and leaning. Red wax hardened over the wood beneath like petrified tears. Four of the objects were shriveled and dried like prunes, but the one to the far right, was much larger, still red enough to identify and oddly almost fresh enough to beat. Davey stared, and though he wasn't aware he did it, gasped the name "Rose."

40

Days went by since their grim discovery and the question came as to the whereabouts of their own hearts. Davey had made the suggestion that those in the barn were theirs, but Ben insisted they weren't, that according to the books, or Maggie's notes—he couldn't remember which—those who still walked could only do so if the organ was wrapped in an item belonging to them.

Opportunity rose one afternoon while Maggie was out on the tractor, taking in the cool breeze under a merciful sun. Ben and Dave combed over the entire ground floor, second floor and attic. Their search had turned up nothing. They took turns at the windows, keeping a close eye on Maggie as she tilled under the remains of harvested crops, while Ronny played outside in the sandbox Ben had built for them—a new battleground for the plastic soldiers.

Finally, the search took them to the cellar where neither could stand guard at the ivy-covered windows. They would have to go by noise alone, listening for the tractor. The basement was dank and smelled of dirt and filled with all manner of boxes, bags of old clothes, furniture under dust cloths, moldering crates full of old magazines and newspapers and even a dressmaker's dummy. Dusty shelves lined the walls filled with jars meant for canning.

Near the back was a tapestry hung by rope that upon further inspection hid a door to another room. The two went through and searched until Davey opened the door of an old oven and found a bath towel folded in half, faded pink and orange. Resting on top were three bundles wrapped in various material. The first was fist sized and wrapped in white cloth that had once been a shirt sporting the faded and cracked remains of an iron-on decal that read *Grandma spoils me.* Ben picked it up and pulled the fabric free from the dried blackened muscle inside.

Upstairs in the living room, as the cartoon rabbit outwitted the stammering hunter, Ronny gasped and shivered. In his chest something began to buzz. The rabbit kissed the hunter and ran away and Ronny giggled, but his eyes stayed wide and fearful.

The second heart was wrapped in a piece of denim from a jacket, while the third in plaid flannel. Ben had never felt such a mixture of joy and sadness as at that moment. They picked up what was theirs and went up the creaking steps, the tractor still announcing that all was clear.

41

Davey sat finishing up the Ed Gorman western he was reading as Ronny lay on the floor watching cartoons. Ben slouched in the recliner and pretended he was asleep.

"I gotta run in town, be gone a few hours. Gotta get feed and groceries, then got an appointment with Dr. Hardy. I'll be home before dark. Thinking, we'll have spaghetti for dinner." Maggie leaned into Ronny's smiling face, "Except for you, Ronny. I'm makin' your plate with worms and blood instead of noodles an' sauce." She cackled as she dug her fingers under his arms and tickled him into hysterics.

"We'll get the barn work outta the way 'til you get back," Davey assured as he hugged her.

"That's fine. You finish your cowboy book?" She stopped and looked back at Davey.

"Just about, I'll have it done by bedtime."

"Maybe I'll stop by the book mill and see if I can find you a new one." With that she winked and made her way out the door and down the steps to the waiting truck.

As soon as she turned out of the mouth of the lane, Ben looked at Davey and coughed to get the boy's attention. The boy looked over the top of his book and the man nodded. Davey gave a sigh full of grief, laid the book on the sofa arm and nodded back. They stood and left the room, and Ronny never took his eyes off the television.

42

It took them less than an hour and a half to dig the three holes, and they spoke very little while doing so.

"Good idea about the ice cream and the videos. Ronny'd be upset he knew what we was up to." Davey said, between gasps as he poured shovelfuls of dirt onto the mound.

Ben nodded and wiped the sweat from his forehead onto his sleeve. "I managed this last night while in bed." Ben opened his shirt. His chest was gaping, a cavernous dark red beyond. His sutures hung from the opening like so many fish hooks from the maw of a shark. "We need to get you and Ronny open. It stings some, but no blood, no mess. If need be we could even close 'em back ourselves. In case Maggie shows before we…"

The words were too profound to speak. Neither of them wanted to talk on it or hear about it. It just needed done.

"So we just put them back in and that'll break it? The spell or whatever?" Davey asked.

"That's how I read it. Then I figure we'll just die. Then and there." Ben smiled and it was a bright smile, honest as children. "I'm tired, boy, I wanna move on. I'm missin' something inside of me, and it ain't just my heart. I hope we all find what we're missin'. That's my hope."

Davey clenched his jaw, gritted his teeth.

Anything to stop the tears that most certainly were coming, a fit that felt like it may never stop if he let it come even for just a quick moment.

Ben poured the last bit of dirt on the pile, laid his shovel down and walked to the porch. Davey did the same, picking at the sinew that held his chest closed along the way.

43

"C'mon, Ronny. Let's go out to the barn and play in the hay," Davey said, turning off the television just as the coyote was painting the mouth of a tunnel on the stone side of a cliff.

"Okay but when I start gettin' itchy I wanna quit, okay?"

"Sure thing." A lump sat in Davey's throat like a stone, and he followed the younger boy as he bounded out the door and down the porch steps. Ben followed them with their hearts cradled in his arms. They came around the barn and Ronny saw the trio of graves behind it. He stopped and looked at Davey.

"What're them holes for?"

"Us" Davey answered, his voice was a weak thing that held too much pain. He grabbed Ronny under the arms. Ben stepped in and pulled the boy's shirt up, exposing a long scar that ran the length of his breastbone. He pulled the stitches free and Ronny screamed. Ben held his small, withered heart in his fist like a softball.

"Ronny. You just be still now. This ain't gonna hurt you, and God, boy, you've earned it. You deserve to be at peace and Davey and I are going too, right behind you. So we'll be together, I swear to ya. This here is what's meant to be." The boy stopped squirming and sobbed with no understanding.

"What about Mama?" he asked, a tiny bubble of

snot puffed in and out at his nostril like a bullfrog's sac.

"She ain't your mama, son. She's a nice lady, she means well. But she ought not be doing what she did." Ben leaned close until his nose touched the young boy's. "I love you, you know." And with that he pushed his fistful of heart into the small chest and pulled out his empty hand quickly. Ronny went silent and sat down hard on the ground. His eyes stopped their tears and he almost smiled.

"I'm Stephen Bates. I have a Mom and Dad. I got a little sister who picks her nose and eats it and a dog named Luker." He began to talk slower and his speech slurred. "I was born in July 1977. We have a pool at our house. My Dad has a motorcycle..." With that, he slumped on his side and was still.

Davey could not speak through his crying, and that was fine with Ben, he was busy crying himself. They lowered the small boy in the shortest hole and laid him flat. They worked together to cover him over. Then Ben looked to Davey. "You're up," was all he managed, a heavy hand on the boy's shoulder. He gave a small squeeze.

"Fair enough." Davey stepped down into the medium sized hole and opened up his shirt. He pulled the rest of the sinew free and dropped it in the soil beside him. He pushed his hardened heart home, with a sharp inhale. He looked at Ben and held out a shaking hand, which the man took and held for what seemed like hours.

"You're a brave and good boy, Davey. Look for me and Stephen when you get home."

Davey laid back and closed his eyes. "My name is Christopher," the boy whispered. A whisper that cracked and fell into crying. "I can't remember anything else." The boy's crying grew quiet until he fell still, Ben looking down over him. After a few long minutes, Ben replaced the soil and smoothed it with the flat of the shovel.

44

Ben walked into the house and let the door bang closed behind him. He stomped up the stairs and gathered all the books he could carry from Maggie's shelves and threw them onto her bed. He grabbed armfuls of shirts and sweaters from her small closet and added them to the pile. He took a lighter from her night table, one with a large-mouth bass jumping out of the water, free from any hook, and set the bedding on fire. He waited for the flames to start devouring the books and clothing then went downstairs. He gathered the books that were on the tables and floor and threw them on the couch. He yanked down the curtains and tucked them under the books and then tied them together and laid it out to the bottom of the stairs like a long fuse. He then touched butane flame to the upholstery until it sizzled and burned. He stood for a while and let the smoke and heat dry his stinging eyes. When the house was a fury of flame and roar, he turned and walked out onto the porch. He was a pearl against the darkness of the smoke rolling behind him. He walked off the porch and towards the barn. Behind him, timber groaned as it turned to cinder and ash.

With thick tongues of smoke rising into the cataract sky above, Ben sat down slowly and opened his shirt. He picked up the remaining heart from the ground beside him and pulled open the flesh of his chest, and his ribs like a door, showing his heart its rightful place. He mumbled and then began to cobble together a prayer. "Oh, Lord, Welcome us home." He pushed his heart into its cradle, as gently as if it were glass. He gasped and spoke as loud as he could: "Welcome me, Lou, home. Wrap us in wing and silver. Kiss our hurts and heal our hearts."

Lou looked down at his hand, at his tattooed finger. He didn't rub the spot but caressed it, with a gentle thumb. This time it did spark good memories. He then pulled as much dirt into the grave as he could, covering himself up to the shoulders.

"Let her know how sorry we are." He managed to pull a little more dirt over himself, working his shoulders under the loose soil, shaking his head until the dirt began to fall upon his face. As the clods of earth obscured him from view almost completely, he fell still.

High above the graves, buzzards began to circle and the sun its slow retreat.

Muffled by the soil was a final sound that might have been "Amen."

———

Author Notes

A few years ago John sent me a short story he'd written called *Maggie's Farm*. Barely a sentence is written between us that the other doesn't read, and there are a few reasons for that. One is that we're honest with each other. If something isn't working then we say so, brutally if need be. The other is that our heads are often in the same place. We share the same heartache. We miss the rocky relationships we had with our fathers (who died within the same year). We get hurt by and pissed off at the same things. John yells at me to be patient sometimes, and sometimes I need to yell it back. While John writes with more of a poetic slant, our topics and interests are similar enough that it just works. The collaboration you just read was inevitable.

With *Maggie's Farm*, John was looking for feedback before he sent the story out for hopeful publication. What I read was the best story he'd sent me thus far, and with a little cleaning up I knew he'd have an easy time finding it a home. He subbed it, and it was rejected. I was bummed for him but pointed out that it was just too short and had the potential of being a novella. I encouraged him to add more, a lot more. He said he tried but felt he was ruining it, taking the life out of it somehow.

John sent *Maggie's Farm* out again. At this point, I flat out told him I *hope* it gets rejected. I said that because I knew he had something much better than a 3,000 word story to be hidden away in an anthology few eyes would see. The story was rejected a second time. He said he was done with it for now and put it back in his folder of slush. That's when I offered to help. I had some ideas on lengthening it, developing the characters, creating new ones, and adding a handful of scenes I thought would liven it up. So he handed it over to me. I told him that if I had to write another 15,000 words on my own that I would, because the initial idea of the story was pure gold. It was just too small a space for the crushing impact the ending could offer if expanded on.

After I'd added a few thousand of my own words, I put it on hold while we both finished individual obligations and current works in progress. Come July 2018, I brought *Maggie's Farm* out again, poked John with it and shared with him my ideas. This time he was ready to join me in fattening it up.

He was nervous at first. But once scenes were thrown together, new characters were developed and old ones brought to life, John adored it and became very proud of the work we'd done. Both our hearts, our souls. They're in here together. And without the one, there wouldn't be the other. Thanks for reading.

~ Chad

John Boden lives a stones throw from Three Mile Island with his wonderful wife and sons. A baker by day, he spends his off time writing or watching old television shows. He likes Diet Pepsi and sports ferocious sideburns. He's a pretty nice guy. His work has appeared in *Borderlands 6*, *Shock Totem*, *Splatterpunk*, *Lamplight*, *Blight Digest*, the John Skipp edited *Psychos* and others. His not-really-for-children children's book, *DOMINOES* has been called a pretty cool thing. His other books, *JEDI SUMMER WITH THE MAGNETIC KID* and *DETRITUS IN LOVE* are out and about. He has a slew of things on the horizon.

Chad lives in Battle Creek, MI. with his wife, children. For over two decades, he has been a contributor to several different outlets in the independent music and film scene, offering articles, reviews, and artwork. He has written for *Famous Monsters of Filmland, Rue Morgue, Cemetery Dance,* and *Scream* magazine. His fiction can be found in a few dozen magazines and anthologies. In the summer of 2016 he released his dark coming-of-age novella *OF FOSTER HOMES AND FLIES* which has been praised by authors Jack Ketchum, James Newman, and many others. The release of *FLIES* began a trend of heartfelt, yet dark, novellas with *WALLFLOWER, STIRRING THE SHEETS,* and his most recent, *SKULLFACE BOY.* Chad can be found lurking the Internet at **www.chadlutzke.com**.

Thanks to...

Robert Ford, Kristi DeMeester, Michelle Garza, Matt Weber, Mary Lutzke, Karen Boden, Duncan Ralston and Shadow Work Publishing, Zach McCain, Connie McNeil Bracke, Dan Padavona, Dean M. Watts, Dyane Hendershot, George "Book Monster" Ranson, Liane Abe, Linda Lutzke, Michael Perez, Shannon Everyday, Shaun Hupp, Steve Gracin, Steven Gomzi, & Tim Feely.

1983: A boy and his little brother wander through a loosely stitched summer. A summer full of sun and surrealism, Lessons of loss and love. Of growing up and figuring it out. Nestled in the mountains of Pennsylvania is a small town, it's not like the others. Things are strange there—people die but hang around, pets too. Everyone knows your name and sometimes, a thing as simple as a movie coming to the local theatre, is all it takes to keep you going.

————

"JEDI SUMMER drops the floor right out from under you, leaves you standing in a childhood that's been roiling around inside your chest for too long. But you'd trade anything to stay there just one more day." ~ **Stephen Graham Jones, author of** *MONGRELS* **and** *AFTER THE PEOPLE LIGHTS HAVE GONE OFF*

"It moved me more than any novel in recent memory. Highly, highly, highly recommended, and I'm almost certain it will be one of the ten best books I'll read this year. Mark my words—John Boden is a writer you're going to want to read so that five years from now, when everyone is raving about him, you can say, 'Oh, I've been reading him for years'." ~ **Brian Keene, award winning author of** *THE RISING, PRESSURE* **&** *THE COMPLEX*

A neglected 12-year-old boy does nothing to report the death of his mother in order to compete in a spelling bee. A tragic coming-of-age tale of horror and drama in the setting of a hot New Orleans summer.

"Original, touching coming of age." ~**Jack Ketchum, author of** *THE GIRL NEXT DOOR*

"Disturbing, often gruesome, yet poignant at the same time, Chad Lutzke's OF FOSTER HOMES AND FLIES is one of the best dark coming-of-age tales I've read in years. You'll laugh (sometimes when you know you shouldn't), you'll cry, you'll find yourself wondering how soon you can read more of this guy's work. Highly recommended!" ~ **James Newman, author of** *MIDNIGHT RAIN, ODD MAN OUT,* **and** *THE WICKED*

"OF FOSTER HOMES AND FLIES by Chad Lutzke is a lovely addition to the coming of age subgenre. He creates in the character of Denny an authentic young man with passions and foibles, someone easy to relate to and root for. The novella hits all the right notes you expect out of a coming of age tale, while also providing a plot that has originality and surprises." ~ **Mark Allan Gunnells,**

author of *FLOWERS IN A DUMPSTER* and *WHERE THE DEAD GO TO DIE*

"...one of those real treats that comes down the pipe and manages to get you all excited about reading again...the whole thing is just beautiful." ~ **Ginger Nuts of Horror**

"Of Foster Homes and Flies is the darkest, most disturbing story Chad Lutzke has written. It's also his best...the ultimate one-finger salute to oppression...Highly recommended." ~ **Dan Padavona, author of CRAWLSPACE, QUILT and STORBERRY**

"...a brilliant coming of age story. This isn't your average horror book...a masterpiece." ~ **Horroraddicts.net**

The world will end.
In a myriad of ways.
Meet Allan, harvester of souls.
Witness rebirth in an old junkyard.
Behold murder and chaos and revelation.
Nightmares swirl and bait. Insects scurry.
The dominoes are all in line.
The world will end.

In bloodstains and beauty.
Watch sweet little children in sacrifice.
Gaze up at the living clouds.
Follow the St. Vitus dance of the damned.
Screaming sights and faithful mutiny.
The dominoes are falling down.

———

"I've long been in awe of John Boden's ability to distill profound dread into a single propulsive line of prose. With sentences that take your breath away like amplified drumbeats in a dirty nightclub." ~ **Bracken MacLeod, author of STRANDED, 13 VIEWS FROM THE SUICIDE WOODS and COME TO DUST.**

"Dominoes —what would happen if Dennis Etchison wrote a children's book. Don't hesitate to snap this up." ~ **Kevin Lucia, author of THINGS SLIP THROUGH and DEVOURER OF SOULS**

"*Dominoes is the kind of book a homeless English teacher might teach to a classroom of self-assembled dolls he's set up in the middle of a forest. Behold murder and chaos and revelation.*" ~ **Max Booth III**, **author** **of** *HOW TO SUCCESSFULLY KIDNAP STRANGERS* **and** *TOXICITY*

An elderly funeral home worker, struggling with the loss of his wife, develops an unnatural attraction to a corpse that resembles his late bride in her younger years. A story of morbid desperation, loneliness, and letting go.

"Stirring the Sheets is a disturbing tale of loss that both tugs at your heartstrings and turns your stomach." ~ **Zach Bohannon, bestselling author and co-owner of Molten Universe Media**

" Lutzke writes of insurmountable grief as if it's an old acquaintance, drawing the audience into a story they can't put down. Heart wrenching and touching." ~ **The Sisters of Slaughter, Bram Stoker Award nominees/authors of** *MAYAN BLUE* **&** *THOSE WHO FOLLOW*

"Stirring the Sheets is a mesmerizing and believable tale of lost love and a broken protagonist...a haunting tale of a man come undone by grief. Lutzke has a keen grasp of the dark psychological elements of bereavement." ~ **Duncan Ralston, author of** *WOOM* **and** *SALVAGE*

"STIRRING THE SHEETS is a bittersweet meditation on grief, loss, and mortality. Chad Lutzke's prose sings in this somber tale." ~ **Todd Keisling, author of *THE FINAL RECONCILIATION* and *UGLY LITTLE THINGS***

"Heartbreaking, somber, and damn tense when Lutzke unleashes his dark side. Stirring the Sheets will affect me for many years." ~ **Dan Padavona, author of STORBERRY & CRAWLSPACE**

"…a short, but extremely effective, character portrait of loss, loneliness, and despair. I'm again surprised at Lutzke's ability to draw a character so distinctly with so few pages to work with." **~The Horror Drive-In**

"Heart-wrenching and powerful. Be warned: this emotional story will stay with you long after you've finished it." ~ **Armand Rosamilia, author of the *DIRTY DEEDS* crime thriller series**

Detritus is young, a little odd, and in love with a dead girl who doesn't know she's dead. Detritus? best friend is also a ghost in a Nazi costume. These things are strange, but nothing compared to the dark and surreal wave rolling toward him. He needs to be ready. The Opposite is coming.

———

"At times poetic and petal delicate, and at other times dangerous and razor sharp, Detritus In Love is the type of delicious little story you'll want to gobble up in one sitting." ~ **Kristi DeMeester, author of** *BENEATH* **and** *EVERYTHING THAT'S UNDERNEATH*

"With Detritus in Love, Mercedes M. Yardley and John Boden have created a beautifully poetic dark fantasy of love, loss, and belonging that will break your heart and leave you haunted." ~ **Damien Angelica Walters, author of** *PAPER TIGERS* **and** *SING ME YOUR SCARS*

"What unfurls in the form of The Opposite is a haunting and unsettling presence--one that our protagonist, Detritus, must battle, with a motley crew consisting of only his ghostly best friend and a long dead love. Suits of skin, bloody rain, vermin and insects unified in upheaval--this tapestry is a vibrant, visceral horror, written by

two introspective visionaries." ~ **Richard Thomas, author of** ***BREAKER* and *TRIBULATIONS***

"My name is Levi. I'm 16. I've got a skull for a face. And here's how shit went down."

Having never been outside the walls of Gramm Jones Foster Care Facility, sixteen-year-old Levi leaves in the middle of the night with an empty backpack and a newfound lust for life. A journey that leads him into the arms of delusional newlyweds, drunkards, polygamists, the dangerous, and the batshit crazy. His destination? Hermosa Beach, California where he's told there is another like him, with the face of a skull.

"This is Huck lighting out for the territories, and kind of documenting an era for us on the way. Only—because it's now not then—he's got a skull face to deal with. As do we all." ~ **Stephen Graham Jones, author of MONGRELS & MAPPING THE INTERIOR**

"I'll show up for anything this author writes...something magical happens on these pages." ~ **Cemetery Dance**

"Lutzke dazzles with his heartfelt stories into strangeness, but Skullface Boy is in a league of its own. His story of Levi, a disfigured

boy with a golden soul, taking a road trip to find his father is a masterwork." ~ **Lee McGeorge, author of** *SLENDERMAN, SLENDERMAN, TAKE THIS CHILD*

"Chad Lutzke has done it again!" ~ **Horror Novel Reviews**

After an encounter with a homeless man, a high school graduate becomes obsessed with the idea of doing heroin, challenging himself to try it just once. A bleak tale of addiction, delusion, and flowers

---

"Lutzke creates a dark vision of a realistic horror. It's beautifully told and powerful…" ~**Splatterpunk Zine**

"It's gripping and tragic, and very excellently written."~**Mark Allan Gunnells, author of WHERE THE DEAD GO TO DIE**

"…a novella rich in character development."~Char's Horror Corner

'Powerful. Moving. Bleak…A great book by a great author." ~ **Shaun Hupp, author of MANIACS WITH KNIVES and POUND**

"Chad gets inside the human existence, turns it inside out, and nails it to the wall." ~ **Mark Matthews, author of MILK-BLOOD and BODY OF CHRIST**

"Chad has a knack for writing believable, grounded characters dealing with honest problems, fears. Wallflowers is no exception." ~ **Zachary Walters, The Eyes of Madness**

For more Delicious Dark Fiction, visit
www.ShadowWorkPublishing.com